Night Caller

Clint awoke with a start. There was someone in the room with him.

He heard something then. A soft, swishing sound, like cloth rubbing cloth. Someone was moving across the room toward him, rapidly, quietly.

It was time to reach for the gun, but as he did so, he felt something fall down around his neck. He closed his hand, but it closed on air as the thing around his neck tightened and whoever was holding it pulled him back, away from the gun.

As he fell off the bed backward, he couldn't breathe. He was still off balance as the intruder pulled on him. He dug his heels into the rug, but there was not enough purchase for him to resist.

So he decided to stop resisting. . . .

Also in THE GUNSMITH series

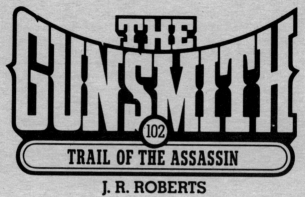

THE GUNSMITH

102

TRAIL OF THE ASSASSIN

J. R. ROBERTS

JOVE BOOKS, NEW YORK

TRAIL OF THE ASSASSIN

A Jove Book/published by arrangement with
the author

PRINTING HISTORY
Jove edition/June 1990

ISBN: 0-515-10336-5

Jove Books are published by The Berkley Publishing Group,
200 Madison Avenue, New York, New York 10016.
The name "Jove" and the "J" logo
are trademarks belonging to Jove Publications, Inc.

PRINTED IN THE UNITED STATES OF AMERICA

10 9 8 7 6 5 4 3 2 1

ONE

When the summons came to Labyrinth, Texas, from Washington, D.C., Clint Adams was not there. The clerk at the office, never having gotten such a telegram before—his hand started shaking when he found out who it was from—wasn't quite sure what to do with it. In the end he decided to take it over to Rick's Place, since Clint spent a lot of time there.

T.C. opened the front door of the saloon and accepted the proffered piece of paper. He knew it was a telegram, but he didn't know who it was for. The clerk simply handed it to him and walked away, happy that his duty had been discharged.

When T.C. unfolded it and started reading, *his* hands began to shake. He immediately decided that it was time for his boss, Rick Hartman, to wake up.

At that moment Rick was in bed with Wanda June Winestock, a blonde in her twenties who had been working for him for just two weeks. She was tall and slender, with small but perfectly rounded breasts and long, graceful legs. She was two inches taller than he—and more than that when she wore heels—but he was not intimidated by her height, as most men were. Rather, to him it was a challenge. Besides, women are all the same height in bed.

It was early and they were busy waking each other up when there was a knock at the door.

Rick had Wanda June's buttocks in his hands, pulling her close to him and driving himself even deeper inside of her with every thrust. She had her legs stuck straight up in the air and spread wide for him, and she was moaning into his ear. The way she stuck her legs up like that excited him, because he'd never had a woman who had done that before—and because they were so damned *long*!

"What the hell—" Rick said when the knocking persisted. "Who the hell is it?"

"It's me, boss," T.C., the black bartender, said.

"T.C.," Rick said, trying to be patient, "I'm not awake yet."

"Oh," Wanda June said into his ear, licking it and making him shiver deliciously. "I am!"

"Shhh!" he told her.

"Boss, I'm sorry to bother you, but I've got a telegram."

"Slip it under the door."

"It's for Clint."

"T.C.," Rick said, "Clint is not in here with me."

"I know that, boss," T.C. said, "but it's from, uh—"

"From who?" Rick asked.

"From the president of the United States."

"The president!" Wanda June said.

Rick withdrew from Wanda June and got to his feet. He walked to the door and opened it, unmindful of his nakedness.

"Where is it?" Rick asked.

"Here," T.C. said.

"Did you read it?"

"I had to," the black man explained, "to see if it was important enough to, uh, wake you."

"All right," Rick said, "all right, T.C. I'll see you downstairs."

"Sure, boss."

Rick closed the door and went back to sit on the bed. Wanda June leaned against him, her hard nipples pressing into his back, and looked over his shoulder.

"What does it say?" she asked excitedly.

He held it close to his chest and said, "I don't know if I should show you. It's probably classified."

"I'll classify this," she said. She reached around and cupped his testicles, then slid her hand up his still erect penis.

"All right, all right," Rick said. "Let's see what it says together."

CLINT ADAMS

REQUEST YOUR PRESENCE IN WASHINGTON, D.C., SOON AS POSSIBLE.

RUTHERFORD B. HAYES
PRESIDENT OF THE UNITED STATES

"Is that really from the president of the United States?" Wanda June asked.

"I guess it is," Rick said, thoughtfully.

"And who's Clint Adams?"

"A very good friend of mine."

"And he knows the president?"

"Well, I don't know that he's ever met him, or his predecessor, but he has served them in several different capacities."

"Like how?"

"Well, a while back he babysat some visitors from another country."

"What country?"

"Russia."

Wanda June shrugged, as if she'd never heard of it.

"Another time he changed his appearance and his name to try and find some killers."

"And this man's a friend of yours?"

"Yes," Rick said. "His name is Clint Adams, but he's also known as the Gunsmith."

Wanda June looked surprised. "That name I've heard."

"And," Rick continued, "he's done some work for the Secret Service."

"The what?"

Rick decided he was better off ignoring the question. He had something else on his mind.

In the past he knew that Clint had been contacted by his friend Jim West and, on occasion, by the head of the Secret Service himself.

If he was being contacted now directly by the president of the United States, it must be for something *very* serious.

Now, if he could just remember where Clint was . . .

TWO

Clint Adams rode into Garland, Kansas, with the feeling that something was waiting for him. He didn't know what it was. The feeling was not even particularly good or bad. It was just a feeling that . . . *something* was ahead of him.

What he *knew* was ahead of him was a job. The sheriff of Garland was a friend of his named Sam Elliott. Sam had sent a message to Clint in Labyrinth, saying that he needed his help, and Clint was always ready to help a friend, no matter how much trouble he'd already gotten into in the past by doing the same thing.

He left Duke at the livery stable and walked to the hotel, carrying his saddlebags and rifle. Garland was a small town but a growing one: He could see that just during that short walk. He didn't know how the people were, but maybe Sam Elliott had found himself a home.

Elliott had been a lawman all his life, but most of that time he'd been a federal marshal, moving around and being sent wherever he was needed. Elliott was now in his early fifties and was ready to stop traveling.

7

He had gotten this job in Garland about six months before. And now Clint had a telegram from him, asking him to come to Garland.

"I need help" were the last three words on the telegram, and those were the words that Clint Adams had never been able to keep himself from responding to—especially when those words came from a friend.

He entered the hotel and found himself in a small but tastefully furnished lobby. The clerk behind the desk was wearing a black suit and tie with a boiled-white shirt. He smiled at Clint before he even reached the desk, and Clint found himself quickening his pace, as if trying to save the man some smiling time.

"Can I help you, sir?"

"Sure," Clint said. "I need a room."

"Certainly," the man said. "Just sign the book, please."

Clint signed in.

"And how long will you be staying, Mr. Adams?"

"I don't know."

"Here on business?"

"Not really."

"What is it you are here for?"

"Do these questions come with the room? Or do I *not* get the room if I don't answer the questions?"

"I'm sorry, I'm sorry," the man said quickly. "I'm just too nosy. I meant no offense."

The man was young, in his early twenties, and was probably just curious.

"That's all right," Clint said. "I didn't mean to snap at you."

"That's all right," the clerk said. "Here is your key, sir. Enjoy your stay."

"Thanks."

Clint took the key, picked up his gear, and went up the stairs to the second floor. He found his room in front of the building, overlooking the main street.

He tossed his saddlebags onto the bed, leaned his rifle against a wall, and walked to the window. His intention had been to ask someone the way to the sheriff's office, but he saw now that it wouldn't be necessary. He could see the office from his window, diagonally across the street.

He wanted a drink and something to eat, but he thought he'd better go over and see Sam Elliott before he did any of that.

The sign next to the door said "SHERIFF SAM ELLIOTT." It had been professionally hand-painted by someone. Clint knocked on the door and walked in.

"Clint!" the sheriff said, before Clint had even closed the door behind him. Elliott got up from behind his desk and walked toward Clint with his hand out. "You made it."

"Sure I made it, Sam," Clint said. He took the hand and found the handshake firm, but that was virtually all he recognized about the man.

It was almost seven years since he had last seen Elliott, and in that time his friend seemed to have aged twice that much. Never a tall man, he had thickened around the middle considerably, and he looked shorter than Clint remembered. His hair, once thick and wavy, was now gray and thinning. His face, once a robust pink, had grown pale and lined.

"I know," Elliott said. "Some change, huh?"

"Sam, I—"

"That's all right, Clint," Elliott said. "I know I've changed a lot."

Clint squeezed the man's hand and said, "It's good to see you, Sam."

"Good to see you too, Clint," Elliott said. "From the look of your clothes you just rode in, eh?"

"Just minutes ago, as a matter of fact."

"Want to freshen up? Get a drink and something to eat?"

"If you can take me this way, I'd like to get a cold beer and something to eat."

"Come on," Elliott said, grabbing his hat. When he turned away, Clint could see the bald spot on the crown of the man's head.

"I'll buy," Elliott said, turning back and putting his hat on, "and I know just the place."

"Hello, Sheriff!" The woman who spoke was in her late forties, a handsome woman who had once been a lovely woman. She was not tall, and she had started going toward plump, in a big way. Her breasts were full and firm, and her hips and buttocks were straining at her skirt. Her black hair was streaked with gray. Her eyes, however, were probably unchanged. They were so blue and so lovely that they couldn't have been any lovelier.

"Clint Adams, Molly Todd," Sam Elliott said. "Molly makes the best meal in town."

"I'll bet it didn't take you long to find that out," Clint said to Elliott.

"The first week he was here," Molly said. "You fellers want some dinner?"

"Your best, Molly," Elliott said. "Your very best."

"How about starting with a couple of cold beers?"

"Sounds good to me," the sheriff said.

"I'll bring them to your table, Sam."

"*Your* table?" Clint said as they walked toward it. "*Your* lady?"

"Well," Elliott said, "I'm trying."

They sat down at a corner table that seemed significantly separated from the rest of the tables in the place. About half the other tables were filled, and Elliott had exchanged greetings with several people on his way to his table.

Molly appeared with two frosty mugs of beer and said, "Dinner will be served soon, gents." She briefly laid a hand on Elliott's shoulder before leaving.

"It doesn't look to me like you'll have to try very hard, Sam," Clint said, picking up the beer. He cut some of the trail dust in his throat and put the mug down half-empty.

"Want to tell me why I'm here, Sam?" Clint asked.

"Old friends don't get a chance to chat before they discuss business?"

"*Business?*"

Clint could remember when the word *chat* was not anywhere near Sam Elliott's vocabulary.

Elliott drank some beer, licked his lips, and said, "All right. I've been the sheriff here for about six months now. In that time I think I've done a pretty good job."

"Knowing you, I'm sure you have," Clint said.

"It's taken me a while to settle into the job, you know."

"After all the traveling you've done, I can understand that."

"The first month, though, I guess I was a little irritable. I mean, being off the trail takes some getting used to."

"What are you driving at?"

"I had some trouble the first month I was here with some drovers."

"What kind of trouble?"

"They were horsing around, shooting up some of the buildings, breaking some furniture. . . ."

"Doesn't sound too unusual."

"Then they started pushing some of the people around—a couple of women. The husbands objected, and they pistol-whipped one of them."

Clint remained silent, waiting for Elliott to finish on his own steam.

"Well, I had to put one of them down."

"Killed him?"

Elliott nodded.

"What's the problem?"

"The other three men with him—two of them were his brothers."

"What'd they get?"

"Six months."

"When are they getting out?"

"Within the next couple of weeks."

"And they're coming back?"

Elliott nodded.

"Don't you have any deputies?"

"One," Elliott said, "but he's strictly for checking doors and windows at night."

"So, hire some others."

"I intend to," Elliott said, "but I need someone to back me up now—or within the next couple of weeks."

Clint stared at his old friend and touched his finger to his own chest.

"Yes, you," the sheriff said. "What do you say?"

Clint shrugged and said, "Why not? I'm here, and I've got nothing better to do, do I?"

After they had finished dinner, Elliott asked Clint to meet him at the saloon in a couple of hours. Clint took the opportunity to go back to the hotel, have a bath, and get some fresh clothes on. Maybe he'd even get a shave.

As he started up the steps to his room, the clerk called out to him.

"I have a telegram for you."

"A telegram?" he said, frowning. Only Rick Hartman knew where he was. Why would Rick be sending him a telegram?

He came down off the foot of the steps and walked over to the desk to accept the telegram.

"Something important?" the clerk asked.

Clint looked the man in the eyes and said, "When I know, you'll be the very next person I tell."

Clint took the telegram up to his room to read it. After he had read it once, he read it again, and it still said the same thing.

He frowned and folded the telegram.

What had he said to Sam Elliott about having nothing better to do?

THREE

Walking to the saloon to meet Sam Elliott, Clint didn't know what he was going to say. When he got there, he decided to simply tell Elliott the truth and see where they went from there.

The saloon was of medium size and had been fixed up very nicely. The bar was well polished, and there were a couple of crystal chandeliers hanging from the ceiling. It was a modest place, but someone had sunk some money into it.

From the looks of things, though, the money was coming right back. They were doing a brisk business: There was a roulette wheel and a faro table, and there was no space available at either.

As for the bar, Clint had to elbow his way up to it, but a space finally opened up—just enough for him to order a beer.

"Comin' up," the bartender said.

When the man returned with the beer, Clint asked, "Has the sheriff been in tonight?"

"Not yet," the bartender said. "Should be in soon, though. Got a problem?"

15

"No."

"Friend of his?"

"Yes."

"Go back a long way?"

Clint stared at the man and said, "Is everyone in this town nosy?"

The bartender blinked and said, "Hey, I didn't mean no offense. Uh, I got other customers."

"You'd better go and take care of them then."

The man nodded and moved further down the bar, glancing back at Clint nervously.

Clint knew that the man hadn't meant any harm, but he was on edge at the moment. He had to do something that was very difficult, and he wasn't looking forward to it. He did not like to disappoint an old friend like Sam Elliott.

Clint was working on his second beer and watching the play at the faro table when Elliott entered the saloon. He saw Clint and waved for him to meet him at the bar. When Clint got there, Elliott already had a beer in his hand.

"How do you like this place?"

"Pretty busy."

"And it'll get busier," Elliott said. "This town is growing, Clint, and I'm gonna be part of it."

"Sam," Clint said, "can we go somewhere quieter?"

"What's the matter, getting old? You don't like the noise?"

"No, it's not that," Clint said. "I have something I want to talk to you about."

Elliott stared at Clint for a few moments, as if trying

"Will they all be accompanying us when we, uh, see the city, sir?"

"Oh, I don't think so," Rashi said. "Just my wife, myself, my personal aides—"

"Personal aides?" Caroline asked, interrupting him.

Rashi gave her a quick look.

"I'm sorry to interrupt . . ." she said.

"That is quite all right," Rashi said, stiffly. "I understand that American women have a certain . . . independent quality. It is something I will have to learn to deal with while I am in your country."

Clint could see by the look in Caroline's eyes that the remark did not sit well with her, but she held her tongue.

"Is there something about the phrase 'personal aides' that interests you?"

"Yes," she said. "Judging from their appearance, I'd say they were more like bodyguards."

Rashi smiled at Caroline and said, "They perform many functions, but they all 'aid' me."

The smile he gave her was an amused one, and she chose that moment to stare into the fire.

Clint had the distinct feeling that Viktor Rashi, for all his good manners and charm, was never going to be one of her favorite people.

SEVENTEEN

Clint told Rashi that they would leave him to rest after his trip and be back in the morning to talk. Rashi insisted that they join him for breakfast in his suite and Clint said that they'd be happy to.

What Clint really wanted to do was get Caroline out of the room. Chandra and his twin showed them to the door.

Once in the hallway, Clint asked Kelly, "Has Green gotten me a room on this floor?"

"Yes, sir, room three-fourteen," Kelly said. "Right there."

It was not directly across from Rashi's room but diagonally across.

"Here's your key," Kelly said, taking it out of his pocket.

"Thanks. I'll go down and bring up my gear."

Clint went downstairs with Caroline and then stopped outside his door.

"Why don't you go home and get some rest," he said to her.

"Can you imagine the nerve of that man?" she

asked. She'd been quiet on the way down. "He was *amused* by me!"

"Don't let him get to you," Clint said. "He's going to be with us for a while."

She looked at him then and said, "Did you really tell me to go home?"

"I did," he said.

"Do you really mean that?"

"I have to move my gear upstairs, Caroline," he said. "Do you really want Mr. Kelly to see us go into my room together?"

"Why not?" she asked. "He's not going to come in and watch us, is he?"

"Caroline—"

"You're mad because of what happened earlier tonight," she said.

"I'm not mad."

"Then why—"

"Caroline," he said, "work with me on this, will you? We have to be up very early in the morning to have breakfast with the man."

She studied him for a few seconds, then said, "All right, Clint, I'll listen to you . . . tonight."

"Thank you," Clint said, even as he was registering the last part of her statement. She smiled, waved at him, and went to the steps.

When she was gone Clint unlocked the door, wondering how much trouble he was going to have with Caroline after that night.

As he entered he stopped short when he saw someone sitting on the bed.

"Why so surprised?" Kate O'Hara asked. "I heard you wanted to see me."

EIGHTEEN

Clint closed the door and said, "Hi, Kate."

Kate O'Hara, the prettiest red-haired, freckle-faced Colleen Clint Adams had ever had the pleasure of meeting, got up from the bed and gave him a sisterly kiss on the cheek.

"How are you, Clint?"

"I'm fine."

"What are you doing in Washington? Did Cartwright ask you to come?"

"No," Clint said. "Cartwright, I'm sure, wishes I wasn't here. Help me collect my things, will you? I have to move upstairs."

"Why?"

"That's part of why I'm here," he said.

Clint trusted Jim West like he trusted no other man in the world. Jim had trained Kate O'Hara, and sometimes he thought that Jim and Kate had a deeper relationship than just pupil and teacher. He also knew that Jim trusted her implicitly, and for that reason he did, too.

He told her about the president sending for him and why.

"I see what you mean about Cartwright not wanting you here," she said. "That's a slap in the face for his department. Hey, wait a minute!" she said, throwing down a shirt that she was holding. "That's a slap in the face to me, too, isn't it?"

He smiled and said, "Don't take it personally."

Clint had his clothes packed, and he picked up his gunbelt and rifle. He had been carrying his little New Line Colt, not wanting to wear the regular Colt on his hip while walking through Washington. Of course, if trouble did rear its head, he would have liked to have something more powerful than the New Line available to him. He was going to have to see about getting a shoulder rig for the big Colt.

"Let me carry that," she said, taking his bag from him.

"Well," Clint said as they left the room, "if Mr. Rashi could see me now, I'm sure he'd have a new respect for me."

She looked at him quizzically as they started down the hall.

Upstairs, Kelly watched as Clint and Kate walked up to him. Clint knew what he was thinking by the look on his baby face: Clint had left with one woman and was returning minutes later with another.

"Everything all right, Kelly?" Clint asked.

"Uh," Kelly said, swallowing and staring at Kate, "quiet . . . everything's quiet . . . sir."

"Good," Clint said. "Would you see that the desk gets this key for me?"

Kelly put out his hand and accepted the key to Clint's old room.

Clint stuck the key into the door of his new room,

swung the door open, and allowed Kate to enter ahead of him. He went in, first giving Kelly a wide-eyed look, just to give the kid something to think about.

"Oh, my," Kate said, dropping Clint's bag to the floor.

This suite of rooms was identical to the one Viktor Rashi had across the hall, but it was furnished in different colors. Where Rashi's room was done in blues and greens, this one was done in shades of maroon.

"I like it," Kate said, putting her hands on her hips and looking around. "I like it a lot."

"So do I." He put down his gun and rifle and said, "Let's look at the rest of it."

They went through the other rooms, and Kate even sat on the bed, which had the thickest mattress Clint had ever seen.

"I could get to like this," she said, bouncing on the mattress. From any other woman the remark might have sounded suggestive. From *Caroline Munro* it *certainly* would have sounded that way, but from Kate it was simply an honest reaction.

"Are you working on anything now, Kate?" he asked.

"Not at the moment. I finished something up last week and I've just been taking it easy since then."

"Would you like to give me a hand on this?"

"Sure," she said. "Do you think the president would approve?"

"He doesn't have to know," Clint said, "and neither does Cartwright."

"What about your friend?"

"What friend?"

She leaned forward and said in a low voice, "The lady who was so disappointed at being sent home."

"Oh, you heard that, huh?"

"I wasn't eavesdropping," she said, "but yes, I heard it."

"Her name is Caroline Munro."

Kate's eyes widened, and she said, "The Barracuda?"

"Is that what they call her?"

"That's what *everyone* on Capitol Hill calls her."

"Why?"

"Because a barracuda has a lot of very sharp teeth, that's why," Kate said. She squinted at him and lifted her feet off the floor so that they were sticking straight out in front of her, as though she were a little girl. "She hasn't sunk her teeth into you yet, has she?"

"What do you mean, yet?" Clint asked. "Do you think that it would be inevitable?"

"Definitely," she said, laughing.

Clint didn't say anything.

"She has, hasn't she?" Kate said. "No, don't answer that. I don't want to know. To answer your question from before, yes, I'd be happy to help you out with this. What would you like me to do?"

"You know the sources Jim uses."

"Some of them."

"Ask around. See who it was who told him there was going to be an attempt on the president's life."

"All right."

"See if you can find out if the attempt is supposed to be made by someone with the Indian contingent."

"Right."

"Rashi's got twenty-three people in his party. One

of them could very easily be an assassin.''

"Why would India want to assassinate the president of the United States?"

"I don't know," Clint said. "Maybe I should ask Mr. Rashi that question tomorrow morning at breakfast."

"You're having breakfast with him?"

"Yes," Clint said, "Caroline and I both are."

"Maybe she'll let go of you and sink her teeth into him," she said.

"Kate—"

"Never mind," she said, standing up. "I don't want to know."

They went into the main sitting room, and she walked to the door.

"Do you want me to report to you here?" she asked.

"Sure."

"What about Kelly, outside?" she asked. "He's sure to tell Cartwright I was here *and* whenever I come back."

"Has he got a big mouth?"

She sighed and said, "He's young, and he's only been with the Service a little over a year."

"What about this feller Green?"

"Dallas?" she asked. "He's sweet, but he has a lot to learn. Is he in charge?"

"Yes."

"Well, Kelly will tell him that he saw me, and then he'll tell Mr. Cartwright."

"Well, if your reputation can stand the strain," Clint said, "let's just let them think that we're friends."

"But we *are* friends."

"No, Kate," Clint said, "I mean . . . *friends*."

"Oh," she said. She thought that over for a moment, then smiled and said, "My reputation can stand that. In fact, I'm flattered."

"All right, then. Get back to me whenever you find out something."

"Right."

She began to open the door but then stopped and asked, "Should I tell Gloria that we're not really . . . *friends*?"

Clint frowned and said, "I'm not all that sure she'd care, at this point."

"Uh-oh," Kate said. "Did she see the Barracuda?"

"She did," Clint said, "but she was starting to talk funny even before that."

"Funny?"

"The way some women talk after they know a man for a while?"

"Oh," Kate said, nodding, "like *that* 'funny.' "

"Yeah . . ."

"Well, I can see where that would concern you, all right. You know, I think *your* reputation may be taking some strain for a while."

"Don't worry about my reputation," he said. "It can stand almost *anything*."

She smiled at him and said, "I'll see you soon, Clint. It's really good seeing you again."

"Thanks for your help, Kate."

"Hey," she said, opening the door, "what are . . . *friends* . . . for?"

NINETEEN

Clint awoke with a start. There was someone in the room with him—of that he was sure.

He lay still, trying to use his ears to pinpoint the intruder's location. His gun was on the night table next to the bed, but he didn't want to go for it. Not just yet.

He heard something then. A soft, swishing sound, like cloth rubbing against cloth. Someone was moving across the room toward him, rapidly, quietly.

It was time to reach for the gun, but as he did so he felt something fall down around his neck. He closed his hand but it closed on air as the thing around his neck tightened and whoever was holding it pulled him back, away from the gun.

As he fell off the bed backward, he couldn't breathe. It was as if a metal band had closed around his throat.

He reached for his throat and touched what was around it. It wasn't a noose—or at least it was not one made of rope. He tried to get his fingers inside of it, but he couldn't. He was still off balance as the intruder pulled on him. He dug his heels into the rug, but there was not enough purchase for him to resist.

So he decided to stop resisting.

He scrambled to get his feet underneath him and then pushed back. His move threw his attacker off balance just long enough for him to get his hands inside the noose and yank it free.

He had two options then: He could have gone after the man or moved forward and tried to get to his gun. He didn't know who or what he was dealing with, or what other weapons he might have, so he decided to go for his gun.

He bounded over the bed, grabbed the gun, and rolled off onto the other side. He turned around and came up with the Colt held out in front of him.

He waited that way for a few moments, then reached for the gas lamp on the night table. He turned it up high enough to discover that he was in the room alone.

He stood up and padded naked across the floor. Gun in hand, he checked out the other two rooms of the suite before he believed he was really alone.

He went to the door and opened it. The fresh-faced young man outside was sitting on the floor, his head lolling over to one side. He could have been asleep.

Clint stepped out into the hall, still naked, and leaned over the man. He *was* asleep, but someone had *put* him to sleep. As far as Clint could see, the man was healthy enough—he was just unconscious.

Clint walked to Rashi's door and knocked, confident that he was in no danger of waking Rashi himself—if everything were all right. He stood so that whoever opened the door wouldn't be able to see the man sitting on the floor.

One of Rashi's aides opened the door and looked at Clint, showing no surprise that he was buck naked.

"Yes?"

"Is everything all right?"

"Everything is fine, sir."

"I thought I heard something."

"Everything is quiet."

"All right," Clint said. "Thanks."

The man closed the door. Clint looked down at the sleeping man and decided to let him wake up on his own. He went back into his suite, locked the door, and went into the bedroom. On the way to the bed he stepped on something. He bent over and picked up what looked like a kerchief. It felt heavy, though, and he discovered something heavy inside the cloth, placed where it would push against a man's Adam's apple when it was around his neck.

It was an interesting weapon.

TWENTY

There was a knock on Clint's door just as he finished
dressing the next morning. He opened it, and Caroline
walked past him. Out in the hall was another fresh-
faced young Secret Service man who looked as if he
hadn't yet started to shave.

Why, he wondered, was Cartwright entrusting this
duty to men so young and fresh?

"Good morning," he said to Caroline as he closed
the door behind her.

"Good morning."

He noticed now that she was wearing a suit as severe
as the one she wore the first day they met.

She knew what he was looking at and said, "Well,
since you seem intent on keeping our relationship on
a business level, I thought I should dress for it."

"Sure," Clint said, "fine, anything you want."

"I could have dressed in some native attire from
India, but I wanted to keep on showing Mr. Rashi my
American individualism."

"I'm sure he'll appreciate it," Clint said, touching
his neck. When he'd awoken his neck pained him,
and his voice was a little raspy.

"Sore throat?" Caroline asked. "You sound a little hoarse."

"More than you know."

She frowned, approached him, and tipped his chin up.

"*That's* a nice bruise," she said. "Where did you get that?"

"I had a visitor last night," Clint said. "He tried to take my head off with this." He took the odd kerchief from his pocket and handed it to her.

"It's heavy."

"There's something, probably a piece of metal, sewn into the fabric." He took it back and fingered it.

"Who would make a weapon like that?"

"I don't know," Clint said. "Maybe I'll show it to Mr. Rashi."

"But why would anyone try to kill you?"

"Maybe I offended someone yesterday."

"Like who?"

"I offended you."

She gave him a look and said, "That's nothing I'd try to kill you for—at least not with something like that."

"I know," he said, "I was kidding. I don't know who'd want to kill me—at least not here in Washington. I've made plenty of enemies over the years, but I doubt that any of them are here."

"Wasn't there a man across the hall?"

"There was," Clint said, "but he was napping."

"Sleeping?" she said. "He should be fired."

"It wasn't his fault," Clint said, "he was *put* to sleep."

"By who?"

"I assume by the same person who tried to put me out with this."

"But why?"

"I don't know."

She narrowed her eyes at him and said, "Are you sure there isn't something you're keeping from me?"

He smiled at her and said, "Not about this. I have no idea who was in my room last night or why he was trying to kill me."

"How do you know it was a man?"

"Uh, I don't," Clint said. "I assume a woman wouldn't have chosen this particular method to do away with me."

"Really?" Caroline said. "Maybe you and Rashi have more in common than you think."

"Do you really think so?" Clint asked.

"I don't know," she said. "I'll probably have to do some more comparisons."

"Well," he said, "we can start the comparisons over breakfast. Shall we?"

TWENTY-ONE

They left the room and walked across the hall. Kelly was once again at the door.

"Kelly, what was the name of the man who was on duty last night?"

"That was Cord, sir."

"Did he say anything . . . interesting when you relieved him?"

"Interesting, sir?"

"You know, about anything unusual that might have happened during the night."

Kelly thought about it a moment, then said, "No, sir, he didn't say anything to me. *Did* something unusual happen?"

"Stay on your toes, Kelly," Clint said. "Don't let anyone put you to sleep."

"Huh?"

Clint ignored him and knocked on the door. Chandra, the same man who had opened the door for him in the middle of the night, opened it now and looked at him the same way he'd looked at him naked.

"Mr. Adams, Mrs. Munro."

"We're here for breakfast."

"I know why you are here," the man said. "Please, come in."

As they entered Clint said to the man, "Do you ever sleep?"

"Not that you would ever see," the man said, closing the door. "This way, please."

Clint and Caroline exchanged a quick glance and then followed.

When they entered the sitting room Clint almost throught he had entered a restaurant. Rashi had somehow gotten a table and chairs brought up to the room, and next to the table was a tray of food that was emitting enough steam to create a fog. Whatever he had ordered had come extremely hot and still was. In addition to his two bodyguard-aides there was another man standing by stiffly, as if waiting for a command. Apparently, Mr. Rashi carried his own waiter with him wherever he went.

"Ah, my breakfast guests," Rashi said, coming around the table to great them. "Please," he said, taking both of Caroline's hands, "be seated."

The man who had admitted them and another man stood by and would probably stand by as long as it took them to eat. Clint did not see either man ever look at the food.

Rashi held Caroline's chair for her and pushed it in gently behind her. He could smell the eggs and potatoes, and he felt some relief. He was afraid that Rashi might have found some Indian food somewhere and had it brought up.

"I am so glad you decided to come back, Mrs. Munro," Rashi said.

"Did you really think that I wouldn't, Mr. Rashi?" she asked.

He sat in his chair, situated between then, and said with a smile, "Well, I was not quite sure."

Clint watched Caroline, hoping she wouldn't say something that they would all be sorry for.

"Tell me," she said to Rashi, "I only see three chairs. Isn't your wife joining us for breakfast?"

He smiled good-naturedly and said, "My wife is having breakfast in her room, down the hall."

"She has a room of her own?"

"She shares it with my—what is the word you would use? *Concubine? Mistress?*"

Caroline glared at him, trying to decide if he was serious or not. Clint decided to step in between them before fists flew.

"Shall we eat before it gets cold?" Clint suggested.

"Yes," Rashi said, looking at Caroline, "I think so." Finally he took his eyes from her and looked at Clint. "I ordered a big American breakfast. I wanted to try everything."

"I see," Clint said, looking at the tray. There were eggs, potatoes, bacon *and* ham, flapjacks, and biscuits.

"Why don't we get started, then?" he asked. "Mrs. Munro, what can I get for you?"

Caroline looked surprised, but she told Rashi what she wanted, and he filled her plate for her and handed it to her.

Over breakfast they discussed their plans for the day.

"What is it you would like to see first?" Caroline asked.

"Well, I would like to check on the gifts I brought for President Hayes."

"The animals?" Clint asked.

"Yes," Rashi said. "You heard about them?"

"I did," Clint said. "Two cats and a camel?"

"Hardly cats, Mr. Adams," Rashi said. "The finest examples of Bengal tiger and cheetah as you will ever see in India, and a camel. I detected some . . . derision when you spoke of the camel."

"Hardly," Clint said. "I don't know enough about the animal to be derisive."

"I will put this camel up against any horse you would care to supply."

"As what?" Clint asked. "A beast of burden?"

Rashi seemed to take that as an insult.

"Of course, we do use them as beasts of burden," he said, stiffly, "but I would race the camel against any horse you would see fit to produce—for a wager."

"What sort of wager?"

Rashi shrugged and said, "Anything you'd care to bet, Mr. Adams."

Clint thought briefly that if he had brought Duke with him rather than having left him behind, he might have taken Rashi up on his offer.

"You sound fairly confident," Clint said.

"Extremely confident."

"It's too bad my horse isn't here in Washington."

"Is your horse the only horse you would wager on?"

"He's the only horse I'd have enough confidence in to run him against an animal I know nothing about."

Rashi smiled and asked, "How long would it take for you to get him here?"

"Too long," Clint said, but he found himself wishing it were feasible.

Maybe, he thought, if Rashi wanted to see the West . . .

TWENTY-TWO

They agreed that after breakfast they would go and check on the animals. Rashi wanted to see how they had come through the trip before he presented them to the president.

"I'll talk to Mr. Green about the scheduling of your meeting with President Hayes," Clint said. "Also, we'll have to find out where they've taken the animals."

"That's fine," Rashi said.

Clint and Caroline rose to leave, and Rashi stood up and said, "I enjoyed the breakfast, Mr. Adams, Mrs. Munro. Perhaps we can do it again."

Clint doubted it. He had discovered that he didn't like Rashi any more than Caroline did. The man was decidedly too arrogant for his taste.

As they turned to leave the room, Clint put his hand into his pocket and said, "Mr. Rashi, excuse me."

"Yes?"

"Can you tell me what this is?"

He took out the kerchief he'd almost been strangled with and showed it to the man.

Rashi reached out slowly and took it out of Clint's

hand. He stared at it for a moment before he finally replied: "This is a *ramel*."

"A what?"

"It is a weapon used by the *thuggee* cult," Rashi said. "Sometimes it is a cord or, as in this case, a scarf."

"What is a *thuggee*?" Clint asked. Rashi had pronounced it *too-gee*.

"The *thug* is an association or cult of professional killers who kill because they think it is the will of *Kali*." Before Clint could ask his next question, Rashi raised his hand and said, "*Kali* is the goddess of destruction."

"I see."

"*Thuggee*, then, is the system of robbery and murder they practice."

"And how do they kill?"

"By strangulation," Rashi said. "They never spill blood." Rashi looked at the *ramel* in his hand and asked, "Where did you get it?"

"I found it," Clint said.

"Where?"

"On the floor in my room."

"I see."

Rashi stared at it for a few more seconds, handling it very gingerly, and then gave it back to Clint, who asked him, "Could this . . . cult be called by another name?"

"What name did you have in mind?"

"Assassins?"

Rashi thought for a moment. "Yes, that would fit."

"What would they be doing here, in the United States?" Clint asked.

"I am sure I do not know," Rashi said. "Are you sure you *found* this in your room?"

"Quite sure," Clint said, pocketing it. "Why?"

"If a *thuggee* were in your room last night," Rashi said, "you would be dead."

"Would I?" Clint said. "We will come back for you in about a half-hour, sir."

"Very well."

"Oh, by the way . . ."

"Yes?"

"Is it written in stone that you and your aides have to wear those turbans?"

"Why?" Rashi asked, touching his. "Do they offend you?"

"Not at all," Clint said, "but they will attract undue attention."

Rashi stared at Clint and then said, "We will remove them."

"Thank you."

Out in the hall they nodded at Kelly, and Clint asked, "Where is Dallas Green?"

"I believe he's downstairs, sir."

"Good," Clint said, "we need to speak to him."

On the way down the steps, Caroline said, "He's pretty arrogant, isn't he? *And* confident?"

"Yes."

"You don't like him any more than I do, do you?"

He looked at her before saying, simply, "No."

"Are you going to take him up on his wager?"

Clint laughed. "A camel against a horse?"

"*Now* you sound derisive."

"I suppose so," he said. "Everything I know about

camels doesn't lead me to believe they have the speed
to match a horse.''

"And what do you know about camels?"

"Only what I've read."

"Then I'd say Mr. Rashi is in control, as far as a
wager is concerned," she said. "He knows about
camels and horses. If he's willing to bet that a camel
can outrun a horse, *I* certainly wouldn't bet against
him."

"I would," Clint said, "if I had *my* horse here."

"Well, if they stay long enough, maybe you'll get
the chance."

"Maybe . . ."

They found Dallas Green in the lobby, talking to
another young man. Clint reminded himself to ask
Cartwright why he'd sent only young and relatively
new men on this assignment. Cartwright wouldn't like
being questioned, but Clint would throw the authority
of President Rutherford B. Hayes at him. In the face
of that, Cartwright would have no alternative but to
answer.

"Dallas?" Clint said.

Green turned, saw them, said something to the other
man, and then approached them.

"Where are the animals?" Clint asked.

"The animals?"

Clint sighed and said, "The tiger, the cheetah—"

"Oh, and the camel," Green said.

"Yes, the camel," Clint said. "Where are they?"

"The zoo."

The Washington Zoo was fairly new. It was only
six years since the very first zoo, in Philadelphia, had

opened. The city fathers, upon hearing that, thought it important that the nation's capital have one as well.

"Mr. Rashi wants to inspect the animals before he presents them to the president," Clint said. "When is his first meeting with the president scheduled for?"

"Later this evening."

"Dinner?"

"Yes."

"All right," Clint said. "We'll need transportation for Mr. Rashi and his party."

"Are they all coming?"

"I don't know," Clint said, "but my only concern is him. He'll no doubt have his two bodyguards with him and probably others. He and his two men will ride in a buggy with Mrs. Munro, myself, and you. Have your men spread out and cover the others."

"I only have five—"

"I know," Clint said. "If any of his wives come along, cover them first."

"All right."

"Dallas, tell me something."

"What?"

"Have you or any of your men been on the job more than a year?"

Green hesitated a moment. "I've been with the Service for eighteen months. One other man has been a member for over a year, the others for less."

"Did you ask for this assignment?"

"No," Green said, "I have no seniority to be asking for certain assignments."

"Cartwright gave it to you?"

"Yes?"

"And the others?"

"I suppose . . ."

"Did he ask you to pick the other men or did he assign them to you?"

"He told me who I would be working with and that I would be in charge."

"All right," Clint said. "Get those buggies set up out front, will you?"

"How many?"

"Get four," Clint said. "If we need more we'll commandeer them."

"Right."

"We'll be out in twenty minutes."

Green nodded and left to get it done.

"It might not be so bad that he's so young," Caroline said.

"What do you mean?"

"If he were older and with the Service longer, he might resent you."

"What makes you think he doesn't?"

"If he does he's hiding it," she said. "An older hand wouldn't bother."

He nodded, knowing that she was right.

Still, it wouldn't have hurt to have one or two older hands along.

TWENTY-THREE

Clint stared at the camel.

"Beautiful," Rashi said, "isn't he?"

Clint didn't answer. As far as he was concerned the animal was anything *but* beautiful—and it smelled worse than a buffalo!

"Of course," Rashi said, "he lost some weight on the trip, but he still looks magnificent."

The camel was not in a cage but rather was behind a fence, grazing.

Rashi looked at Clint and said, "I would like to get closer so I may examine him more closely."

"Of course," Clint said. He motioned Green to let Rashi into the pen, and Green turned to the zoo representative who was with them.

"This way," the man said.

Clint watched as Rashi entered the pen and began his examination of the camel.

"That is one ugly animal," Caroline Munro said.

"I know."

"And the *smell*!"

"I know."

"I can't wait to see the tiger, though," she said.

"I understand they *really are* beautiful."

"I'm looking forward to that myself."

Clint looked around him at the rest of Rashi's people. They had needed three buggies to accommodate them all. Rashi's two personal bodyguards—he called them "aides"—had gone into the pen with him. Two women had accompanied them, and Clint assumed that one was his wife. It was difficult to see what they looked like, as they kept their faces covered, but their skin was smooth and brown and there was a red mark on both their foreheads. They were both clad in their traditional *sari*. There were two more "aides" standing next to them who had shared the second buggy. There was an older, gray-haired man who Clint had no idea about, and two other men who had ridden in the third buggy with him. All three of them were wearing loose-fitting, native clothes. None of the three looked like they were more "aides."

Clint noticed that one of the women—the more petite of the two—was constantly looking his way, and whenever he caught her she averted her eyes quickly.

"Here he comes," Caroline said.

Rashi approached Clint, who asked, "What's his condition?"

"Excellent," Rashi said. "He looks even better for the lost weight. I would like to check on the tiger now."

"This way," the zoo employee said, and they all followed him. "We put him in a cage by himself."

"Excellent," Rashi said.

"Well," the man said, "we didn't have any other

tigers to put him in with, and we didn't think we should put him in with our other cats."

"If you had," Rashi said, confidently, "you would no longer have any other cats."

They walked the rest of the way in silence until they'd reached the cage with the tiger. Rashi took one look and became perturbed.

"I want that cage cleaned!" he exclaimed angrily. He looked at Clint and said, "That cage is a disgrace."

"We'll have it taken care of," Clint said, eyeing Green, who nodded. "Would you like to go in and examine him?"

"Are you mad!" Rashi said. "He would tear me apart. I will have Hakka do it."

Rashi turned and said something in his native tongue to Hakka, who turned out to be the gray-haired man. The man, short and stocky but powerfully built, walked to the entrance of the cage with the man from the zoo and waited for him to open it, then he stepped inside with the huge Bengal tiger.

Clint was impressed with the size of the tiger. He was much larger than any mountain lion or cougar that Clint had ever seen. Even the big cat he had seen in South America* could not compare with the tiger. The animal had been pacing back and forth, and Clint watched in admiration the play of muscles beneath the tiger's hide.

He watched now as Hakka approached the tiger, speaking to it softly. The animal stopped pacing and

*THE GUNSMITH #29

stood staring at the man. For a moment they stood that way, man and beast just staring, and then it was the tiger who averted his eyes and turned away. Hakka moved forward then and made a quick but close examination of the animal. Then he backed out of the cage. He may have stared the animal down, but he wasn't foolish enough to turn his back on him.

"Hakka is the absolute master of all animals," Rashi said proudly.

"I can believe it," Clint said.

"He's magnificent," Caroline said. She sounded breathless, and her eyes were glowing as if she were sexually aroused. Clint wondered if she meant the tiger or the man.

Once Hakka was out of the cage and the zookeeper had locked it, Rashi said, "And now the cheetah."

They walked as a group to the cage where the cheetah was being kept, and Rashi made the same comment about the dirty cage, only not as vehemently this time.

Once again Hakka entered the cage, stared the animal down, and then examined it. In its own way though on a smaller scale, this animal was every bit as regal and impressive as the Bengal tiger.

While watching Hakka in the cage with the cheetah, Caroline had drifted away from Clint, probably to get a better look at the cat—or at Hakka. Rashi also moved away to get closer to the cage, and Clint became aware of someone moving into his place. He looked to his left and saw one of Rashi's women, the petite one who had been stealing glances at him.

"Hello," she said from behind her veil, and Clint

wondered if she weren't shattering some form of protocol by speaking to him.

"Hello," Clint said.

She barely came to his shoulder. Up close her eyes looked as dark as chocolate. They did not exchange any further words after that, but Clint was aware of *something* going on between them. She was wearing her native clothing, which covered her from head to toe and seemed to have several layers, so he couldn't really tell what kind of shape she had. He *could* see her hands, which rested on the rail in front of them, and they were exquisitely shaped, strong-looking hands for one so small.

She moved away from him suddenly when he became aware of Rashi returning. He didn't know if the man had seen him speak to the woman.

"Well?" Clint asked. "What's the verdict?"

"The animals are all in excellent condition," Rashi said. "If the conditions of the cages will be taken care of, I will be very satisfied."

"Good," Clint said. "You're our guest, and we want to keep you happy."

"I appreciate that."

Hakka came around to speak to Rashi, and Caroline drifted back to Clint's side.

"What did the little lady have to say?"

"You saw that?" he asked. "I thought you were busy looking at the animal."

Caroline threw an unmistakable look Hakka's way and said, "I was . . . but I still saw."

"She said hello."

"And what did you say?"

"Hello."

"And?"

"That was the end of the conversation."

"But not of the *communication*, huh?"

"I don't know what you mean, Caroline."

"Of course not," she said. She looked at Hakka again, who was about fifty but was certainly enough of a man to interest a woman like Caroline. She could appreciate the air of danger he projected.

"I hope he doesn't smell like a camel," Clint commented.

Caroline laughed and said, "I'll let you know, darling."

TWENTY-FOUR

They loaded into the buggies and made the trip back to the hotel.

Clint accompanied Rashi back to his room with Caroline and Green.

"I will see you tonight, Mr. Rashi," Clint said.

"Will you be having dinner with us at the White House?" the man asked.

"Oh, yes," Clint said, "Mrs. Munro and I will both be there."

"Excellent. I will see you then."

"We'll meet you here and ride over with you."

"Excellent," he said again. It was one of the man's favorite words.

Rashi went into his room with his aides, leaving Clint, Caroline, and Green outside.

"Don't forget to keep a man out here at all times," Clint said to Dallas Green.

"I will," the younger man said. "I'm not a stupid man, Mr. Adams. I know something is happening that I'm not aware of."

"I don't know what you mean."

"Sure—"

123

"As a matter of fact," Clint said, before starting off down the hall, "make it *two* men."

"Well," Caroline said to the Gunsmith, "that certainly put his mind at rest."

Down in the lobby Caroline said, "I'm going to go home and pick out something wonderful to wear. I didn't know I was having dinner at the White House."

"Neither does the president."

"What? Hey, wait a minute," she said, "I've crashed some parties in my time, but the White House—"

"Don't worry about it," Clint said. "The president and I are like that." He crossed his fingers.

"Sure . . ."

"Just be beautiful," he said. "That certainly won't be hard for you."

"Why, Clint Adams," Caroline said, "I do believe that was a compliment!"

"Sure sounded like one to me," he said.

"And what are you going to do between now and dinner?" she asked.

"I'm going to have a talk with one of my least favorite people in the world."

"How many guesses do I get?"

"None," he said. "I'm talking about William Masters Cartwright."

"Why doesn't anyone like that man?" she wondered aloud.

"I'll ask him. . . ."

TWENTY-FIVE

Clint went directly from the hotel to C Street and presented himself to see Cartwright.

"Do you have an appointment?" the receptionist asked him.

"Lady," Clint said impatiently, "I don't need an appointment. Just tell him I'm here."

She looked offended and said, "Wait here, please."

She stood up and left him to wait there while she went and spoke to Cartwright. When she came back, she had a look on her face that said "Now you're going to get it," though her voice said only, "You can go in."

"Thanks."

He knew where Cartwright's office was, and he entered without knocking.

"What do you want, Adams?" Cartwright demanded.

"You've got some explaining to do."

"I don't have to explain anything to you," Cartwright said.

"I think you do."

"Why?"

"Because I'm working for the president, Cartwright," Clint said, leaning on the man's desk. "If I don't get all the cooperation from you that you can give me, I'll go straight to the head man."

Cartwright glared at Clint, but he was licking his lips nervously.

"The vice-president—" he started, but Clint cut him off.

"Forget about the vice-president," he said. "I'm talking about the president. Understand?"

Cartwright looked down at his desk—not that there was anything there for him to see, but he needed to look away from Clint's eyes.

Clint looked around for a chair and pulled it over so he could sit across from Cartwright.

"All right," Cartwright finally said, "what do you want to know?"

"I want to know why you assigned a bunch of kids with no experience to guard the visitors from India."

Cartwright frowned. "Why should I waste my experienced personnel on a babysitting job?" he asked. "Green and the others can handle the job."

"There's a little more to the job than just 'babysitting,' Cartwright," Clint said.

"Like what?"

"Like catching a would-be killer."

"What are you talking about?"

Clint took the *thuggee* weapon from his pocket and tossed it onto Cartwright's desk. The metal piece in it made a sound when it struck the top of the desk.

"What's this?"

"Someone wrapped that around my neck last night," Clint said.

Cartwright picked it up, then looked surprised when he felt the weight of it.

"Who?"

"I don't know."

"Was it someone from their party?"

"I don't know that, either, but this weapon is from India."

"Then it *is* one of them."

"Or it's someone who wants us to *think* that it's one of them," Clint said.

"Well," Cartwright said, tossing the thing back into Clint's lap, "you've got enough of my men on the job to work with."

"I need someone more experienced."

"I don't have anyone to give you. Everyone else is assigned."

"What about Kate O'Hara?"

"She's—" Cartwright started, but then Clint saw him stop as though remembering something. He had probably already been notified that Kate had been in Clint's room.

"She's available," the Gunsmith said.

"I . . . have other plans for her."

"Come on, Cartwright," Clint said, "you want me to tell the president—"

"All right, all right," Cartwright said, clearly annoyed. "I'll assign her to you."

"Thank you," Clint said, standing up. "I appreciate your cooperation."

"Yeah . . ."

"Of course," Clint said, "when I catch this jasper I'll make sure you get all the credit you deserve."

Going out the door, he thought he could feel the heat of Cartwright's glare in the center of his back.

In the hall he saw Gloria Manners coming toward him and he stopped. She kept walking, looking down at some papers she had in her hands. She was obviously on her way to Cartwright's office. She was about ten feet in front of him when she finally looked up, saw him, and stopped short.

"Hello, Gloria."

"Clint," she said, folding her arms in front of her. "Are you here to see me?"

"No, Gloria," he said, aware that he might be saying something wrong. "I had to talk to Cartwright about something."

"Oh, I see," she said. "Then this meeting is just an accident."

"A fortunate one, though," he said. "We have to talk, Gloria."

"Now?"

"Sometime over the next few days," he said.

"Well," she said, "I'll look at my calendar and see when I can clear some time."

"Gloria—"

"I have to see my boss, Clint," she said. "Please stand aside."

He stared at her, then shrugged and stood aside to let her pass. She stepped up to Cartwright's door, knocked, and then entered without looking back. He stood there a few more moments before turning and walking toward the front door.

He left the building, hoping that he was not leaving a valued friendship behind.

TWENTY-SIX

Clint went back to his hotel and nodded at the two men who were positioned outside Rashi's door. One of them was Kelly.

Clint went into his room and removed the New Line Colt from his belt. After what had happened the night before, he was going to make it a point of getting himself a shoulder rig before the dinner at the White House. He was also going to need a new suit of clothes for the occasion. He knew that Caroline was going to look no less than sensational, and he didn't want to look like something she had dragged in off the street at the last minute.

He went to the door, opened it, and called Kelly over. The younger man was wearing a very smart suit, and Clint wanted to find out where to go nearby to buy himself a new outfit.

"Come on in for a minute, Kelly."

"Yes, sir."

As Kelly closed the door behind him, Clint said, "I'd offer you a drink, but I don't have anything here."

"Yes you do, sir," Kelly said, interrupting him.

131

"What?"

"I arranged for some liquor to be brought up. It's probably set up in the other room."

Clint walked into the sitting room and saw that a bottle of whiskey had indeed been brought up, as well as two glasses.

"Well," Clint said, "I appreciate that, Kelly. Now will you have a drink?"

"No, sir," Kelly said, "I don't drink."

Clint had been about to pour the man a drink but he settled for pouring himself one.

"I wanted to ask you where I could buy a new suit," Clint said.

"A new suit?"

"Yes, sort of like the one you're wearing."

Kelly looked down at himself, as if to remind himself of what he was wearing.

"I'd settle for someplace near here."

"Well, sir, I believe there is a men's clothing store about two blocks south of here. They have some very nice things there that you could buy."

"Two blocks south, huh?"

"Yes, sir."

"Is that where you buy your clothes?"

"Uh, no, sir," Kelly said, a bit sheepishly, "I have my own tailor."

"Oh, I see."

"I *could* give you his name, if you like . . ." Kelly offered.

"No, no, that won't be necessary," Clint said. "Thanks for the information."

"Of course, sir."

Kelly turned and started for the door, but Clint said, "Hold on a minute."

"Yes, sir?"

Clint wished Kelly would stop calling him "sir." In fact, Dallas Green kept doing the same thing. He didn't need the constant reminder of the difference in their ages.

"Where is the nearest gunsmith's shop?"

"There is a shop a block north, sir," Kelly said. "You can't miss it."

"All right," Clint said. "Thanks. You can go back to your post now."

"Thank you, sir."

As the young man left, Clint finished his drink and closed the bottle. He was more of a beer man than a whiskey man, but since Kelly had thought to get him the bottle he thought it only right he should have a taste.

He picked up the New Line again and tucked it into his belt—hopefully for the last time—and left to outfit himself for dinner at the White House.

TWENTY-SEVEN

After Gloria Manners left his office, William Masters Cartwright sat at his desk, fuming over the way Clint Adams had treated him. Gunsmith or not, who the hell did Adams think he was, threatening Cartwright with the president of the United States?

Cartwright had been making a lot of plans lately for his career, and he wasn't about to allow a two-bit gunman like Clint Adams ruin it for him. Very soon he would be a force in Washington, D.C., and there wouldn't be *anyone*—not even the president of the United States—that Clint Adams or anyone else could threaten him with.

Cartwright decided that he'd sat in his office long enough for one day. The Secret Service could get along without him for the rest of the day. He was going to go to his club, have a big steak and a few drinks, and reflect on the bright future he had in Washington, D.C.

Gloria Manners went back to her office, wondering why she had treated Clint Adams the way she had. They had been friends for a few years now, and that wasn't something to throw away just because he didn't want to be *more* than friends with her. Perhaps she would have to accept Clint Adams as a friend on his terms or give him up totally. She would also have to accept the fact that there were other women in his life—like Caroline Munro, no doubt—but she could be comforted by the thought that he wasn't committing himself to any of them, either.

Clint Adams just wasn't the type of man who was going to settle down with one woman—especially not in an Eastern city like Washington, D.C. He needed to be free, and he needed the wide-open spaces of the West.

So if she knew all that, why was she acting like a child and hiding in her office?

Finally, she decided that the Secret Service could operate for the rest of the day without her. She was going to go and find Clint and make sure that they were still friends.

Caroline Munro picked out her clothing very carefully for dinner at the White House. She would dress in something that was conservative—well, not *that* conservative—but that would at the same time show off her figure to her best advantage.

She wondered if the animal man—that was what she had started to call Hakka, Rashi's animal handler—would be at dinner. She thought back to watching him in the tiger cage and once again—as had happened then—she became moist between her legs. She removed her clothes and stood naked in front of her mirror. She knew she had firm, high breasts and buttocks for a woman her age. Still thinking about Hakka and the tiger, she ran her hands slowly over her breasts, rubbing her nipples with her palms, and then continuing down until one of her hands was pressed firmly between her legs, rubbing up and down. . . .

Hakka was almost as much an animal as the tiger was. Although her ultimate goal was still to once again bed Clint Adams, she wouldn't mind an afternoon dalliance with the thick-bodied, gray-haired man.

She wondered if he were *that* thick all over. . . .

President Rutherford B. Hayes sat in his Oval Office, wondering what progress Clint Adams was making. It was probably too soon to hope that the man had found the would-be assassin by now. Hayes missed his wife, but he didn't dare bring her back to Washington while the danger was still imminent.

He rubbed his hands over his face and then stood up. He had to go and prepare for his dinner that night with his guests from India. Although he hadn't been told anything, he was sure that Clint Adams would be present at dinner. Jim West had spoken highly— *very* highly—of Clint Adams's abilities. Hayes only hoped that Jim West was as good a judge of men as he was an agent. Hayes knew of Adams's reputation as the Gunsmith, but that was a reputation he had forged out West, with a gun.

But a gun was not the measure of a man in Washington, D.C.

Shakti Gaudri, the youngest of all of Viktor Rashi's mistresses and the one he'd chosen to take with him to the United States, was thinking about Clint Adams.

She had not seen many American men in her young life, but of those she had seen Clint Adams was easily the most interesting. For one thing, he was not intimidated in the least by Viktor Rashi, as most men were. Although he was not the most handsome man she had ever seen, he *was* the most attractive.

Rashi did not know it, but while he had been having breakfast with Clint Adams and the woman, Caroline Munro, Shakti—sharing the next room with Serena, Rashi's wife—had overheard his conversation with the Munro woman.

If American women really were independent and they made their own decisions, maybe she—at least while she was in America—should be the same way.

She had taken her first step in that direction by even speaking to Clint Adams at the zoo. She had only said one word to him, and he only the same word to her, but she had detected something in the air between them.

She loved Rashi in a way, but they were, after all, in America to have new experiences, weren't they?

Viktor Rashi dressed for dinner. He would be taking his two aides with him—although they would not dine—and he was taking Shakti, his youngest mistress, and Serena, his wife.

When Clint Adams had shown Rashi the *thuggee* weapon, Rashi had not betrayed his true feelings about it. It dismayed him greatly. There were those in his country who did not favor this trip. They would not be beyond murder to ruin it—although he was sure they would not try to kill him or any of his people.

The cult of the *thuggee* was thought to have been

destroyed forty years earlier by the British, though there had been rumors for years that they still existed. This was Viktor Rashi's first proof of the matter.

Clint Adams, however, would be a perfect target—as would any of the other American men who were assigned to them.

There was one other target who would be perfect if those factions were truly intent on turning this trip into an international disaster.

The president of the United States.

TWENTY-EIGHT

As Clint had expected, Caroline Munro looked . . . *exciting*. Her hair was swept up over her head, exposing a truly graceful—if a tad too long—neck. The gown she was wearing fully exposed the mole on her throat—and the tops of her breasts.

"I *had* intended to dress conservatively," she said to Clint as she entered his suite, "but then I said to hell with that."

"You look marvelous."

"Do I excite you?"

"Yes," he answered honestly.

"Enough to go to bed with me right now?" she asked. "I can be out of this gown in a moment."

"Yes," Clint said, "if we had the time. We don't."

"Oh, pooh!" she said, then she shrugged her elegant shoulders—which were also exposed. "Oh well, maybe later—if I don't get a better offer."

Clint picked up his new shoulder rig, slipped into it, and fitted the Colt into it. He picked up his new jacket and put it on.

"How does it look?"

141

"Very impressive," she said. "I had no idea you could cut such a dashing figure."

"I'm talking about the gun."

"Oh . . . Well, if you leave the jacket open, I guess the bulge doesn't show too much."

"That's what I figured, too. Come on, let's go across the hall."

He opened the door to his suite and allowed her to precede him, then closed the door behind him. Dallas Green and Kelly were both in the hall, and both stared at Caroline with undisguised admiration.

Clint moved past them and knocked on Viktor Rashi's door. It was answered by his ever-present bodyguards—both of them.

"Is Mr. Rashi ready to go to dinner?" Clint asked.

"He will need ten minutes," the man said.

"Good," Clint said. "We'll bring the buggies around front. I will come back for him."

"As you wish," the man said. His attitude made it clear that he did not think they needed Clint's protection for Rashi, not as long as he and his colleague were around.

"Dallas," Clint said as the door closed, "get the wagons. Kelly, stay here."

"Yes, sir," Kelly said.

"Come on," Clint said, taking Caroline's arm, "let's go and check out the lobby."

They walked down with Dallas, who explained that his other men were out in front of the hotel, looking for would-be troublemakers.

"That's good," Clint said.

Clint and Caroline remained in the lobby while Green went outside to fetch the buggies.

"We haven't done very much guide work so far, have we?" Caroline asked.

"I guess not."

"More like bodyguards."

"A little bit of both."

"I'm not a bodyguard," Caroline said. "What am I then, window dressing?"

"What do you mean?"

"I mean, is the only reason I'm along is to hang on your arm?"

"Caroline—"

"The vice-president said I was needed as a guide," she said. "That struck me as funny when he said it. Now it strikes me as even funnier."

"Tomorrow," Clint said, "we are going to have to show our guests around the city. *I* can't do that, Caroline. I don't know the city that well. Tomorrow we'll go where you say and do what you say."

She raised both eyebrows at him and said, "Is that a promise?"

He smiled and said, "Within reason."

She grinned wickedly, and they proceeded to check out the lobby for would-be assassins.

Clint and Caroline once again shared the first buggy with Rashi and his "aides." In the buggy behind them were Rashi's women and *their* two bodyguards. The rest of the party had remained behind at the hotel, including Hakka, the animal man.

"Isn't Hakka joining us?" Caroline asked.

"Hakka is very much at ease dealing with animals," Viktor Rashi said, "but you would not want to eat with him, I assure you."

Clint thought Caroline looked a bit disappointed. It was possible she had dressed for the animal man's benefit, and now he wasn't there to see it.

That was okay with him. She looked so good he was glad *he* was there to see her.

They were conducted directly into the White House without delay, and shown to the dining room. There was increased staff on duty, and they saw to it that everyone was seated. Only then did Hayes enter, and Dallas Green did the honors with the introductions.

"I hope you are enjoying our country so far, Mr. Rashi," Hayes said as they shook hands.

"Very much so," Rashi said. He looked directly at Caroline and said, "I am very pleased with your choice of a guide, Mr. President."

"I am pleased to hear it, sir."

President Hayes walked to the head of the table and sat down. On his right was Caroline, and on his left was Viktor Rashi. Clint was sitting to Caroline's right. He had one of Rashi's bodyguards next to him, while the other sat next to Rashi. Rashi's two women were at the end of the table, facing each other, with a bodyguard next to each.

Dinner was served.

After dinner, Hayes and Rashi decided to go off to another room and have a talk. Perhaps, Clint thought, they'd talk about the very reason Rashi had come to America. Rashi's two bodyguards insisted on coming along.

"You can stay here with the ladies, Clint," President Hayes said. "I don't think anything is going to happen here, in the White House."

"Just the same, Mr. President," Dallas Green said, "I would like to go along."

Green and Kelly had both remained in the dining room, but neither had dined.

"Very well, young man," Hayes said. "Come along."

As the president and his guest left the room, Caroline nudged Clint and said, "I'm going to talk to the women."

"Don't start any trouble," Clint said. "I think Rashi likes them the way they are."

"A little independence never hurt anyone," she said.

Clint had a choice: He could try to talk to the remaining bodyguards or strike up a conversation with Kelly. He decided to sit back down at the table and have another cup of coffee, keeping his eyes on the three women at the other end of the table. Caroline was doing most of the talking, and every so often she looked up at him and smiled. A couple of times she said something to the two women that made them also look at him and giggle. He suspected he was the butt of more than one joke.

After half an hour he began to get impatient, so he rose and began pacing the room. The three women did not seem to be experiencing any problem in maintaining their conversation. The two bodyguards stood very close to the two women of Viktor Rashi.

Clint found himself approaching Kelly, who looked at him and smiled.

"I see you found yourself a very nice suit, sir,"
he said.

"Yes, thanks, Kelly."

"The gun shows rather badly, though," Kelly remarked.

"I know," Clint said. "I want it to."

"It ruins the lines of the suit."

"It tells anyone with any ideas that I'm armed."

"I'm also armed," Kelly said, showing Clint the
gun in his shoulder rig, "but my tailor took care with
the lines of the suit."

"He did a fine job, Kelly," Clint said, "a fine
job." He wandered away from the younger man, not
wanting to pursue any further conversation about the
man's tailor.

After an hour and fifteen minutes, Clint was getting
antsy, but then he heard the men returning. As they
entered the room, it seemed to him that the president
and Viktor Rashi were getting along famously. Rashi's two men walked behind him, while Dallas Green
followed the president closely enough to be in his
pocket.

Rashi caught the attention of his two ladies and
said, "It is time for us to go. Thank our host."

Both women stood up, bowed to President Hayes,
and thanked him.

"You are most welcome," Hayes said. He turned
to Rashi and said, "Please, if I can be of any further
assistance, don't hesitate to call on me."

"You are very kind," Rashi said.

"Mr. Green?" President Hayes said. "Would you
show everyone out, please?"

"Yes, sir," Green said. "This way, please."

Clint touched Caroline's arm as she passed him and said, "I'll be along in a moment."

"All right."

When everyone else had left the room, Clint moved to the president's side.

"Do you have something for me?" Hayes asked.

"Only this," he said, showing the man the *thuggee ramel*.

"What is it?"

Clint explained what it was and how it had come to be in his possession.

"Then you've had contact with the assassin?" Hayes said, excitedly.

"I have had contact with *someone*," Clint said, "but he was after me, not you. This may have simply been some kind of diversion."

"What will you do now?"

"Mrs. Munro and I will show Mr. Rashi and his people around the city tomorrow," Clint said. "I'm afraid I'm just going to have to wait for the owner of this thing to try again."

"And what if he succeeds?"

Clint put the weapon back into his pocket. "Then I guess he can have this thing back."

TWENTY-NINE

When they had returned to the hotel, Clint, Caroline, Dallas Green, and Kelly walked Rashi and his two women—as well as their bodyguards—up to their rooms.

Clint and Caroline stopped at Rashi's door with him and his bodyguards, while Green and Kelly continued on to the ladies' door with their bodyguards. Before the women entered their room there was just enough time for the younger one to throw Clint what he could only describe as a hot-eyed glance.

He hoped he was wrong.

At Rashi's door, Clint said to the man, "If we could get an early start in the morning we will be able to show you much of the city tomorrow."

"Wonderful," Rashi said. "We will be ready."

"How many of you?"

"The same as tonight, I imagine."

"Good," Clint said. The number was not *too* unwieldy to handle.

"Mr. Hakka will not be along?" Caroline asked.

Rashi gave Caroline an amused look and said, "He will be staying in his room on the second floor."

"Why is he on the second floor?" Caroline asked.

"He is a servant," Rashi said, as if the answer were obvious.

"I see," Caroline said.

"Ah, I have offended you again," Rashi said. "You do not have servants in this country?"

"Yes, we did," she said. "We had them for a long time. They were called *slaves*."

"Ah, yes," Rashi said, "we have *those*, as well. Good night, Mr. Adams, Mrs. Munro."

Rashi and his men went inside and closed the door, leaving Clint and Caroline in the hall with Dallas Green and Kelly, who had joined them.

"When do you fellers get relieved?" Clint asked.

"About an hour," Green said. "It's been a long day."

"Yeah, it has," Clint said. He inserted his key into his door and opened it. "Good night."

"Good night," Green said, and Kelly added, "Sir."

Clint looked at Caroline, at her mole and her exposed cleavage, and said, "Good night, Caroline."

She smiled and said, "See you in the morning, Clint."

Caroline said good night to the two Secret Service men and went downstairs—as far as the second floor. When she got there she realized she didn't know what room Hakka was in, so she decided to go all the way down to the main floor and find out.

After all, she *was* dressed to squeeze information from a desk clerk.

• • •

Clint undressed and poured himself a small drink from the bottle Kelly had supplied him. He left the sitting room and went into the bedroom, where he stopped short: He saw that someone was there, waiting for him.

It was Shakti, Rashi's youngest "wife"—or, at least, Clint had begun to *think* of her as Rashi's other wife.

He looked around for a moment, wondering how she had gotten in: How had she gotten past the two Secret Service men in the hall?

Finally he looked at her and asked, "How did you get in here?"

From behind her veils she said, "I move quietly."

"Why are you here?" he asked.

She studied him for a moment with her dark eyes. "I thought that would be obvious."

"Uh, now look . . . Shakti?"

"Yes," she said, "that is my name."

Clint sipped his drink, then put it aside on the dresser. "Shakti, you shouldn't be here."

"Why not?"

"You're Rashi's woman," Clint said. "You're a guest in this country."

"That is more reason why you should treat me . . . properly."

"Have I *not* treated you properly?"

"You have not treated me at all," she said. "You have spoken only one word to me since our arrival."

"As you have to me," Clint said. "I think we both know why."

Since he had not moved, she walked across the room, getting closer to him.

"I think we are both attracted to each other, Clint Adams."

"Shakti," he said, "I haven't even seen your face. . . ."

"Is that important?"

"Well . . . yes—I mean, it's not the *most* important thing, but I *am* sort of curious."

"All right," she said. She reached up and unfastened the veil, moving it away from her face.

Clint caught his breath.

"What is it?"

"You're beautiful."

And she was. Her lips were red, making an erotic contrast with her dark eyes and dark skin. Now that he saw her face, he realized that she was even younger than he had first thought.

"How old are you?"

"Nineteen."

"You look younger."

She smiled.

"I assure you I am fully developed."

He studied her. With the layers of filmy clothing she wore, that was hard to ascertain at the moment.

As if reading his mind, her hands went to her clothing.

"Shakti . . ."

He spoke sharply, and for a moment she hesitated, but then she went on and removed all her clothing, layer by layer. It was the most erotic undressing of a woman he had ever witnessed, and by the time she was done he was very hard.

Her body was exquisite. Her breasts were perfectly formed, round with very dark nipples. The hair between her smooth thighs was straight and black. Her legs were short but graceful, the calves firm. Her flesh was totally without blemish and it had that taut, firm look that young flesh always has. Her hair was caught behind her head with something, and she reached up to undo it, letting it fall around her shoulders. As she did so, her breasts lifted and fell, and he felt himself begin to throb. He was more sexually aroused than he had been in some time—and he knew it was wrong.

"What about . . .'' he started to say, but he stopped when she moved even closer to him. He could now feel the heat she was giving off.

He inhaled her musky scent, and she smelled like no other woman he'd ever been with. There seemed to be a mixture of odors, all of which seemed natural. Her skin had one smell, her hair another, and the fact that she was aroused was giving off another. Together they made a heady and probably unique mix.

"Serena?'' she asked, finishing his earlier question. "She knows where I am. She will say nothing. In fact,'' she said, putting her hands on his arms, "she encouraged me to come.''

"Why?''

"In my country when a man has many women, he spends very little time with each of them. Some of us . . . require more time than he gives us.''

He assumed that meant that as a young woman, she was not getting as much sex as she required. This, then, was an opportunity she could not afford to pass up.

As it turned out, it was one he himself could not turn down, either.

THIRTY

To Caroline, Hakka even *smelled* like an animal—
and that excited her even more.

He had his powerful arms around her, crushing her
to him. The wiry, gray hairs of his chest were scraping
her breasts and her nipples, and she was so aroused
that she could hardly breathe.

After obtaining his room number from the desk
clerk, she had gone to his door and knocked. When
he opened it he had simply stared at her, the way he
probably stared at the tiger or the cheetah.

She made the first move.

"May I come in?"

He hesitated, then nodded shortly and said,
"Come," stepping away from the door. He left it to
her to close the door after herself.

He was bare to the waist, wearing a pair of loose-
fitting pants. His feet were bare. She noticed the wiry
chest hair immediately and even then wondered how
it would feel on her nipples. His chest was like a slab
of stone, and his arms had huge biceps. His legs were
short but seemingly as thick as tree trunks.

She stared at the crotch of his pants, wondering . . .

He knew what she wanted, of that she was sure.
As if to prove her right, he slipped his hands into the
waist of his pants, slid them down, and kicked them
away. He wore no underpants, and even when soft
his penis was very large and thick.

Her breath was beginning to come faster and faster.

Clint touched Shakti, and with that touch he knew
there was no turning back from this course of action.
He was going to have this girl, this *woman*, and he
was going to enjoy every moment and worry about
the consequences later.

As he touched her flesh, he felt her tense and then
relax. . . .

Hakka moved toward Caroline with a speed that
frightened her. He gripped her by the arms, his powerful hands hurting her.

"What—" she started, but abruptly his right hand
hooked into the bodice of her gown and tore it away
from her. Her full breasts bobbed free, and he continued to tear at the dress until he had pulled it in
tatters from her body. She was wearing only a flimsy
pair of underpants, and he quickly tore those away
from her.

They were both naked now, and he released her
and backed away. His penis had begun to stiffen,
swelling before her eyes to an incredible size.

"My god!" she said, staring. Could she possibly
accommodate such an organ without being torn apart?

"Come," Hakka said.

She stared into his eyes and found herself powerless to resist.

She moved toward him, staring at his erect penis. She lowered herself to her knees and took him into her hands, sliding one hand down to cup his testicles. His hand went behind her head, and she felt herself being pushed toward him. She opened her mouth. . . .

Clint cupped Shakti's breasts in his hands, and the girl closed her eyes and moaned. He used his thumbs on her nipples, then leaned over and used his tongue. He slid his hands behind her to the small of her back, and she leaned back as he continued to suck her nipples. . . .

Caroline had taken more of Hakka into her mouth than she would have imagined possible, but abruptly he pulled her off of him, lifted her effortlessly, and deposited her onto the bed. She stared at him wide eyed as he positioned himself between her legs, spreading her apart. Then he bulled into her.

She screamed. . . .

Clint lifted Shakti in his arms, surprised by how light she was. He walked to the bed and put her down, then joined her. One small hand encircled his erect penis as his hands roamed her body. He buried his face in her hair, inhaling its scent, then kissed her neck and breasts. For a moment he nestled his face between her breasts, again taking a deep breath.

"Please," she said, "please . . . now . . . I cannot wait. . . ."

He couldn't wait any longer, either. He moved over

her and lowered himself into her and onto her, until
he was buried to the hilt.

They began to move together. . . .

Caroline clutched at Hakka's thick body mind-
lessly. She had never been pierced this deeply, never
been taken this *brutally*. His chest hairs were rubbing
her nipples raw as he continued to slam into her, and
his odor was that of an animal. His hands were holding
her buttocks and squeezing them mercilessly.

Shakti had already shuddered with orgasmic delight
twice, and Clint was most of the way toward an ex-
plosion of his own when he gave in to an overwhelm-
ing desire. He withdrew from her, despite her
muttered protestations—at least he *assumed* she was
protesting, since she was speaking in her own lan-
guage and he didn't understand anything but the tone.

He slid down until his face was between her legs,
and then he began to taste her. Her odor there was as
heady as elsewhere, and soon he was lapping at her
avidly, causing her to ball the sheets up in her hands
and lift her hips off the bed.

After a few moments of that she began to grab at
him, trying to draw him back up to her. He finally
relented and mounted her again, taking her in longer,
harder strokes this time, as she wrapped her short but
powerful legs around him.

Clint didn't know what Rashi's other women were
like in bed, but he couldn't imagine that any one of
them could be any better than this.

• • •

When Hakka withdrew from Caroline she looked at him in confusion. She knew that he had not finished, so she didn't understand why he would withdraw. But then his powerful hands gripped her hips and he flipped her over onto her stomach, and she *knew* what he wanted.

"Wait," she said, "wait, ohhh!"

He spread her buttocks and drove into her and, God help her, she could no longer tell the pleasure from the pain. . . .

Shakti was now astride Clint, riding his rigid penis up and down. She had her hands behind her, bracing her, and his hands were on her breasts, kneading them, pinching her nipples, as she rode him in a frenzied, mindless way, driving herself toward pleasure without the slightest thought of his . . .

And that was fine with him.

THIRTY-ONE

Later Clint and Shakti lay together on his bed, staring at the ceiling, each alone with private thoughts.

Clint was wondering how he would explain this to the president.

Shakti was not wondering about consequences at all—not at this point.

Not yet.

Caroline lay on her side, aware of Hakka's breathing beside her. She felt . . . completely used up. She felt as if she had just run five miles. She was still trying to catch her breath, even though Hakka had fallen asleep ten minutes before. Her legs felt so weak that, even though she wanted to leave she didn't think she would make it to the door on her own. Of course, all she had to wear was her tattered dress, so she was probably going to be stuck here all night with a man who was obviously her sexual superior.

God, his stamina was *incredible*!

She had not thought that she had a male equal sexually. She had been with some women who were her equal but never a man . . . not until this week. Clint

Adams was the first man she had ever been with whom she regarded as her equal. Now she had met the first man who could ever outdo her in bed.

She rolled onto her back and caught her breath. She was sore everywhere but especially from being taken from behind by him. And yet, as much as everything hurt, she knew that she had known sensations— *heights*—this night that she had never known before.

Folding her arms across her breasts, she knew that now she was experiencing the depths.

"Your skin is darker than his," Clint said to Shakti. "Darker than Serena's, too. Also, your name doesn't sound . . . Indian."

She smiled in the darkness.

"My father was Indian, but my mother was African."

"Black?"

"Yes," she said. "I am aware that for a long time blacks were slaves in this country. Does it make a difference to you that I am half black?"

"None at all," he said. "I'm impressed with what the two races have produced. You are the most exquisite creature I have ever seen."

She rolled toward him and kissed his chest.

"Be careful," she whispered. "I do not often hear words like that. I might decide to stay."

He slid his arm around her and cupped one breast, brushing the nipple with his thumb. She rolled on top of him and began to kiss his chest, licking his nipples. She worked her way down to his belly with her tongue, leaving wet patches along the way—long ones, short ones. Her tongue felt like satin on his skin, and his penis was reacting, swelling, growing, until suddenly she was *there*. Heat engulfed him, and he wrapped his fingers in her black hair, which had fanned out across his thighs and belly like a curtain of silk.

Hakka woke Caroline during the night and rolled her over. She began to protest but quickly became aware that something was different. His hands on her breasts felt different, gentler. His mouth on her nipples was loving, not brutal. And when he kissed her for the first time—their previous unions having been completed *without* benefit of a kiss—his mouth was soft, his tongue timid.

When he entered her this time it was slowly, inch by inch, and when he started to move it was slowly, with none of the urgency, none of the *brutality*, he had previously exhibited.

It was as if she were in bed with a totally different man. Everything about him had changed—everything but one small item.

The stamina was still there.

Shakti slipped from the bed and got dressed in the dark. Clint almost let her leave without asking her something that was on his mind. She sat on the bed and leaned into him, and they shared a long, deep, loving kiss. He cupped her face in his hands, staring at her in the darkness.

"Shakti, I want to ask you something."

"Then ask," she said. "I will answer as best I can."

"Someone tried to kill me last night."

"I am sorry!" she said, touching his face. "Were you injured?"

"No, but I am concerned."

"That it will happen again?"

"That someone will try to kill my president," he said. "Someone from your country."

"From my country?" she repeated. "Why do you say such a thing?"

He showed her what had been used in the attempt on his life.

"*Thuggee!*" she said, breathlessly.

"What do you know about them?"

"Only that they are supposed to have been eliminated years ago."

"Is there anyone in your party who might have a reason—something personal or political—to want to kill the president of my country?"

She took a moment before answering.

"I know very little about politics, Clint," she said, "your country's or mine, and I do not know everyone who was brought on this trip. I can only tell you that neither Viktor Rashi nor Serena nor myself would have any reason to kill you or your president."

"What about the bodyguards?"

"I am sorry, but I cannot say."

"All right," he said. "I'm sorry I had to ask you."

"What of Hakka?" she said. "You have not asked me about him."

Clint put his hand to his throat and said, "If it had been him last night, I don't think I'd be here now, Shakti."

"Well," she said, kissing him quickly, "then I am glad it wasn't him."

She stood up and began to leave the room, but she stopped at the door.

"Clint?"

"Yes."

"If the *thuggee* do still exist, and they are after you, they are fanatics! They think they kill for the god *Kali*."

"That's what Rashi told me."

"There is another name for *Kali*. It is *Kunkali*."

"What does that mean?"

"Man-Eater. You *must* be careful."

"I will be."

"I will pray to the god *Vishnu* for your safety."

"Thank you, Shakti."

She said good night, then melted into the darkness.

It was a few moments later that Clint wondered how she was going to get back to her room without being seen.

When Caroline awoke the next morning, she found that she was alone in bed. She rolled over onto her back, spread her arms and legs, and took stock of her body parts. They were all there, they were all working, and they all ached—but the ache was not *totally* unpleasant.

She felt fine. Although the night had not begun the way she'd anticipated—she had *never* lost control of a situation that way before—it had turned out better than she might have expected after their first experience. She had seen Hakka brutish and selfish and had then seen him gentle and loving. All in all, she was still fascinated by the man.

She rolled to the edge of the bed and sat up. That

accomplished, she stood up. Her legs felt weak, but she remained upright. While she was standing there, the door opened and Hakka walked in.

"I brought you some clothing."

"Thank you."

He walked to the bed and dropped a bundle of clothing onto the bed. She could see right away that it was Indian clothing, probably borrowed from one of Rashi's women.

"I can't wear—"

"You must wear something," the man said.

Caroline thought it odd that this was the first time she noticed that the man was several inches shorter than she was.

He was right, though. She had to wear something, or she couldn't leave the room. She looked down at what was left of her gown and knew she couldn't wear that.

"All right," she said, reaching for the clothes.

For the first time Hakka smiled and said to her, "You will look lovely."

She stared at him, wondering which of the men who'd had her the night before was the real Hakka.

THIRTY-TWO

When Clint awoke the next morning he didn't feel well. There was an ache in his belly the likes of which he had never experienced before. When he moved to get off the bed, the ache became a pain, and he doubled over on the edge of the bed, holding his stomach.

At that point there was a knock at his door.

He tried to get up, didn't make it, then tried again and managed to stand. He staggered across the bedroom to the door frame and leaned there, catching his breath. The knock came again, more insistent this time, and he hoped that whoever it was would not leave before he could get there. He had the feeling that he was in serious trouble.

He pushed away from the door frame and staggered through the second of the three rooms in the suite. He wished now that he had never moved from his other room. At least the bed would have been closer to the door.

He reached the door and leaned against it. Perspiration was dripping from his nose and chin to the floor.

"Are you sure he didn't leave the room?" he heard a woman ask.

"He should still be in there, ma'am," a man replied.

I'm still here, he thought. He reached for the doorknob, but his hand was so slick with sweat that he couldn't turn it. He wiped his hand on his thigh and grasped the knob again. This time it turned, and he swung the door open.

"Wha— Clint!" Kate O'Hara said. "Jesus, you could get dressed before you answer the—Clint, what's wrong!"

He was falling—he *knew* he was falling, probably dying—and the last words he heard were someone yelling, "Catch him!"

His mouth felt dry, like a desert.

His eyes felt gritty, as if they were full of sand.

His belly felt empty.

He was alive.

"I'm alive," he said, his voice a harsh rasp.

"Yes, you are," a man's voice said.

He opened his eyes and looked up at the man.

"I'm Doctor Summers. Would you like some water?"

"Yes."

The man put a hand behind his head to support him and held a glass to his mouth. The water tasted better than anything he'd ever had.

He seemed to remember Kate O'Hara's voice. . . .

"Kate . . ." he said.

"Miss O'Hara is outside. Would you like to see her?"

"Y-yes . . ."

"I'll send her in."

"Doc?" Clint called.

"Yes?"

"What happened?"

The doctor, a young man in his early thirties, smiled and said, "I'll let her explain it to you."

The doctor left, and Clint kept his eyes on the door until Kate O'Hara came in.

"How are you doing?" she asked. She approached the bed and took his hand.

"I've been better."

"You could have been a lot worse," she said. "You scared me half to death, opening the door buck naked and then falling into my arms."

"Did you catch me?"

"I had some help from Kelly and Green."

"They were there?"

"Yes."

"Kate . . . what happened? Am I sick?"

"*Sick* is not the word for it," she said. "Clint, you were poisoned."

That stunned him.

"Poisoned? How? With what?"

"Well, they don't know how, and they don't exactly know what with."

"Well, what *do* they know?"

"Only that whatever it was you, apparently you didn't ingest very much of it—*just* enough to make you feel sick."

"Jesus," Clint said, "and just a little makes me feel like *that*. . . ."

He shuddered, thinking what would have happened if he'd had *more* of the stuff.

Where had he been poisoned? At the White House dinner? Was he the *only* one?

"The president—" he began.

"I thought of that, Clint," Kate said. "He's fine."

"Then it didn't happen at dinner?"

"What else have you had?" she asked. "What have you had very little of?"

"I haven't had . . ." he started, but then he stopped short.

Something that he'd had very little of!

"Kate," Clint said, "I want you to go to my suite. . . ."

THIRTY-THREE

Kate went to the hotel and walked down the hall to Clint's suite. Dallas Green and Kelly were still there.

"How is he?" Green asked.

"He's alive."

"What happened to him?"

"Somebody poisoned him."

"Poisoned!" Green said, incredulously. "With what? When?"

"That's what I'm going to find out," she said. Using the key Clint had given her, she let herself into the suite and closed the door behind her.

And she *locked* it!

She went into the sitting room and looked around for the whiskey bottle Clint had told her about. She found the tray and the glasses that had been brought up with it, but there was no bottle.

Someone had removed it.

"Damn!" she swore, looking around.

She looked at the tray again and then leaned over and examined the glasses. Sure enough, one of them had a small amount of whiskey at the bottom. She picked up the small glass, palmed it, and left. The two men in the hall never saw what she was carrying.

Clint was pulling his boots on when Kate entered the room. He was wearing some clothes that Green had collected from his room.

"What are you doing?"

"Did you get it?"

"You're not supposed to be—"

"Did you get it?" he asked again.

"No," she said, "the bottle wasn't there, Clint. Someone removed it."

"Hell!"

"I did, however, get a glass that you used. Hopefully there's enough whiskey left in the glass for them to find out if that's where the poison was."

"Good girl!" Clint said. "When will they know?"

"I gave it to the doctor. He said they'll know very soon."

"I'll wait, then," he said, sitting up on the bed with one boot on and one boot off.

Kate approached the bed, got down on one knee, and grabbed his other boot.

"*We'll* wait here," she said. "Give me your foot."

About twenty minutes later, the door opened and the doctor walked in. Clint was still seated on the bed, Kate in a nearby chair.

"Doc?" Clint said.

Doctor Summers looked at Clint and Kate and then nodded.

"The poison was in the whiskey. How much did you drink?"

"I don't think I had a whole glass."

"The glass Miss O'Hara brought me?"

"Yes," Clint said, remembering that the glass was just a little larger than a shot glass.

"Well, that explains it, then," Summers said. "You ingested just enough so that you weren't incapacitated. If you *hadn't* been able to get to the door when Miss O'Hara knocked, you would probably be dead by now. I'd say this young lady saved your life—in more ways than one. You should be very grateful."

"I am," he said.

"I'll make sure he shows me how grateful he is, Doc," Kate said.

Summers nodded, then seemed to notice that Clint was dressed.

"You really shouldn't be leaving yet. You'll continue to feel some affects for a few days."

"I have things to do, Doc," Clint said. "I've got people to see."

"I'm sure you do," the doctor said. "I'll sign you out, Mr. Adams."

"Thank you, Doc, for everything."

When the doctor had left, Clint looked at Kate and asked, "What kind of gratitude did you have in mind?"

"Dinner," she said, giving him a quick smile. "All I meant was dinner."

Clint said, "You've got yourself the biggest dinner I can buy you once we wrap this up."

"Are we close to wrapping this up?"

"Very close," Clint said. He stood up and wavered there for a moment, feeling slightly dizzy.

"Are you all right?"

"Fine," he said, closing his eyes for a moment. "I'll be fine. Where's my gun?"

She opened the drawer of the table next to his bed and handed him his gun and shoulder rig. He slipped the rig on, checked the gun to make sure it was loaded, and then said, "All right, let's go and wrap it up."

"Who are we going to see?" she asked as they moved toward the door.

"The man who gave me that bottle of whiskey."

THIRTY-FOUR

Clint and Kate hurried back to the Presidential Hotel, hoping to find Dallas Green and Kelly still on duty outside Viktor Rashi's suite.

"By the way," Clint remarked as they entered the hotel, "I haven't ever heard Kelly's first name."

"It's Dan, I think."

"What do you know about him?"

"Not much. Of all the agents we have, he's the newest one."

They went up to the third floor, and Clint became concerned when he saw that the hall was empty.

"Damn!" he said.

They hurried to Rashi's door and knocked, but there was no answer.

"Could Caroline have come and taken Rashi for a tour on her own?"

"It's possible," Clint said. "If she did, Green and Kelly are probably with them."

"Is Rashi in danger?" Kate asked as they went back down to the lobby.

"I don't think so," Clint said. "I think somebody

175

wants to kill the president, then blame Rashi and his people.''

''That's why they attacked you with that weapon?''

''A *ramel*,'' Clint said. ''Maybe I wasn't supposed to be killed—not *that* time, anyway.''

''And this time with the poison?''

''I don't know,'' Clint said.

In the lobby they looked around but could find none of the Secret Service agents who'd been assigned to Rashi's protection.

Clint went to the desk and asked the clerk if he'd seen Rashi and his party leave. The clerk said that they had left about an hour before.

''Where do we look?'' Kate asked.

''I don't know,'' Clint said. ''If you were going to take someone on a tour of the city, where would you start?''

She shrugged and said, ''The Lincoln Memorial, the Washington Monument, the usual places.''

''Well, we'll just have to try the usual places, then.''

''Should we get help?''

''From who?'' Clint asked, giving her a pointed look.

''Cartwright, of course. He can give us some men.''

''Men I can trust?'' Clint asked. ''Like Dan Kelly?''

''I . . . don't know.''

''Kate, right now the only person I trust is you,'' Clint said. ''Are you with me?''

''Sure I am,'' she said. ''Let's go.''

They went outside and got a buggy. Kate told the

driver to take them to the Washington Monument.

"What I can't figure," Clint said, "is why Kelly didn't try for the president at dinner."

"Maybe there was no opening," Kate said. "Maybe he wants to kill Hayes *and* get away."

Clint rubbed a hand over his face.

"He's working for someone," Clint said.

"What makes you say that?"

"It's a feeling I have," Clint said. "He's too young to be doing this for some moral or personal reason. He must be doing it for money."

"Is he working alone, then?"

"That I don't know," Clint said, "but I'd guess not. There's got to be at least one other person involved in this."

"Why?"

"Green has the men working in two shifts," Clint said. "They'd have to have someone on each shift."

"What about Rashi's people?" she asked. "Is one of them involved, do you think?"

"How else would they get their hands on a *ramel*?" Clint asked. "Yeah, I think somebody in Rashi's camp is bought and paid for."

"Well, if Kelly, his accomplice, *and* someone from Rashi's party are all bought," Kate asked, "*who* did the buying?"

"That's something we'll ask Kelly when we find him."

"Do you think he'll talk?"

"The man poisoned me, Kate," Clint said, coldly. "Believe me, when I find him, he'll talk."

• • •

They tried the Washington Monument first, and when they didn't find anyone there they moved on to the Lincoln.

"I see some people," Kate said.

"Well, if Rashi brought along all the people he took to the zoo, they'd make a small crowd."

Clint saw them too, a bunch of people standing in front of the huge figure of the seated Lincoln.

"It's them," he said, recognizing the *saris* worn by Shakti and Serena.

The driver stopped the buggy, and Clint was out before it came to a full stop. He was running toward the group of people, looking for Kelly. He saw Dallas Green, but he didn't yet see the man he wanted.

Kate shouted something from behind him, but he continued on. Dallas Green turned and saw him. He said something to his men, who all had their hands in their jackets.

Clint also drew the attention of Rashi's bodyguards, who moved closer to their boss.

"Clint—" Green began.

"Where's Kelly?" Clint asked hurriedly.

"What?"

"Kelly, Dallas—where is he?"

"He's around," Green said. "He and two other men are checking the area. What's going on? I thought you were in the hospital."

"I can't explain now, Dallas," Clint said, "but I believe that Kelly is the man who poisoned me."

"What? Why, for chriss—"

"We can talk about *why* later, Dallas. Let's find him first."

"All right," Green said. He turned to his three men

and told them to find Kelly and the other two.

"Kate," Clint called out, "stay with Rashi." The Gunsmith then looked at Chandra and said, "Keep a sharp eye on your boss!"

Chandra nodded and moved even closer to Rashi.

Caroline called Clint's name, but he ignored her and moved away from them with Dallas Green.

"Do you think Kelly is after Rashi?" Green asked.

"I think Kelly and whoever's behind him have a bigger target in mind."

"The president?" Green asked, aghast.

"Yes."

"But . . . we were at the White House—"

"I don't have all the answers, Dallas," Clint said, "and I probably never will, but we've got to find Kelly and get what answers we can."

Suddenly they heard shots. Clint pinpointed the direction from which they'd come and changed his course, Dallas Green in tow. They both had their guns out now.

They worked their way around behind the Lincoln Memorial building and saw Kelly trading shots with Green's men. The other two men who had been with Kelly looked confused and didn't know who to fire at.

"I want him alive, damn it!" Clint said.

Green shouted "Hold your fire!" several times before his men finally listened.

It occurred to Clint that none of these men were very good shots. They were all out in the open, but none of them had been hit.

Dan Kelly was standing alone, holding his gun ready. There was a panicked look on his face.

"Don't come any closer!" he shouted at Clint.

Kelly apparently knew that the game was up. He had probably started shooting first.

"Ease up," Clint said to Green.

Clint tucked his gun into his belt and showed Kelly his empty hands.

"Take it easy, Kelly," he said. "No one wants you dead. We just need some answers."

"Don't come any closer," Kelly said. He pointed his gun at Clint but his hand was shaking. Clint doubted that the man could have hit him except by sheer blind luck.

"I know some of it, Kelly," Clint said. "You gave me that poisoned bottle of whiskey."

"That wasn't my idea!"

"I'm sure none of it was, Kelly," Clint said. "Not the poison, not the attack in my room, and not the plan to kill the president."

Kelly stared at Clint and asked, "How did you—"

"The president knew there was going to be an attempt on his life, Kelly," Clint said. "That's why he sent for me. I'm here to stop you and the man you work for. Who is that man, Kelly? Who do you work for?"

"I can't—"

"Look around you, Kelly," Clint said.

Kelly did. Green had apparently given his men some hurried instructions, and they had formed a circle around Kelly and Clint. They all had their guns out. Clint hoped that no one would fire, because as bad as they were with their guns, he figured he had as good a chance of getting hit as Kelly did.

"You can't get away, Kelly," Clint said, "and

there's no point in your taking the blame for everything.''

Kelly was nervously trying to look at all of the men around him at one time.

''You're working with someone, aren't you?'' Clint asked. ''And the two of you work *for* someone— someone who provided you with a contact *inside* Rashi's party. That's how you got this.'' Clint took the *ramel* out of his pocket.

Kelly stared at the scarf in Clint's hand.

''Come on, Kelly,'' Clint urged, ''don't go down alone. That's not brave, and it's not loyal—it's just plain stupid.''

Kelly's gun hand was wavering even more now, and Clint felt he was getting to the young man.

''Start small, Kelly,'' Clint said. ''Who's your partner?''

Clint watched Kelly's eyes as they quickly flicked to the man Clint had seen asleep in the hallway the other night, the man he knew as Cord.

''Cord—'' Kelly started to say, but Cord cut him off by firing twice. One of the bullets hit Kelly and took him down.

Clint drew his gun and said, ''Cord! Hold it!''

Cord turned and tried to bring his gun to bear on Clint, but the Gunsmith fired just once, taking Cord out of the play—permanently.

As several of the men ran to check on Cord, Green and Clint moved toward the fallen Kelly. Blood was pumping from a wound in his chest, and it trickled from his mouth.

''Kelly,'' Clint said, ''you're dying. There's no point in lying now. Who do you work for?''

Kelly's eyes were already glazing over as Clint reached behind him to support his head.

"Come on!" Clint said, shaking him. "Who do you work for?"

Kelly's glazed eyes fixed on Clint. For a moment Clint thought the man had died with his eyes open, but then he opened his mouth and said, "Cartwright," just before a great geyser of blood flooded from his mouth and he died.

"Cartwright?" Green repeated. "Is that what he said?"

"That's what he said," Clint assured him, gently setting Kelly down on the ground. He stared at Green and said, "Why doesn't that surprise me?"

THIRTY-FIVE

When Clint left Washington, D.C., he was anything but satisfied.

William Masters Cartwright had disappeared and was now nowhere to be found. Jim West had been appointed temporary head of the Secret Service, a position he did not want.

Clint now felt justified by the fact that he had never liked Cartwright. The man apparently had a good relationship with the vice-president and he had a plan to put Wheeler in the Oval Office, thereby assuring himself of some position of authority. He had apparently—and this was *all* guesswork—decided that he would never get anywhere relying on his own capabilities as a politician and so had resorted to a planned assassination of the president. When he heard about the visitors from India he very likely felt he had a perfect pigeon to put the blame on. Somehow he had managed to buy someone in Rashi's party. That was the one thing Clint wished he could find out, but he knew he'd never know.

There was no question of the vice-president being involved. Cartwright must have simply felt that with

William Wheeler in power he had a much better chance of advancement.

Both Kelly and Cord were dead, and Clint never did find out who the culprit was within Rashi's party. Viktor Rashi assured him that the man would be ferreted out before they returned to their own country.

Clint was no longer needed as a guide, so that job was left to Caroline Munro, who was apparently *very* fascinated by the animal man, Hakka.

The president had thanked Clint for the job he'd done, and Clint had kept his own displeasure to himself. If the president was happy, that *should* have been all that mattered.

Clint had not gotten another chance to speak to Shakti, which was just as well.

He was in a hurry to leave Washington and get back to Garland, Kansas, and his friend Sheriff Sam Elliott, so he never had another chance to speak to Gloria Manners. He figured he'd have to wait until his next trip to Washington to discover whether or not they were still friends.

He was halfway to his destination before he finally decided to put Washington, D.C., behind him. Sam Elliott needed his help, and he was going to concentrate on that now.

Watch for

SHOOT-OUT AT CROSSFORK

103rd novel in the exciting GUNSMITH series
from Jove

Coming in July!

A special offer for people who enjoy reading the best Westerns published today. If you enjoyed this book, subscribe now and get...

TWO FREE WESTERNS!
A $5.90 VALUE—NO OBLIGATION

If you enjoyed this book and would like to read more of the very best Westerns being published today, you'll want to subscribe to True Value's Western Home Subscription Service. If you enjoyed the book you just read and want more of the most exciting, adventurous, action packed Westerns, subscribe now.

TWO FREE BOOKS

When you subscribe, we'll send you your first month's shipment of the newest and best 6 Westerns for you to preview. With your first shipment, two of these books will be yours as our introductory gift to you absolutely FREE, regardless of what you decide to do.

Special Subscriber Savings

As a True Value subscriber all regular monthly selections will be billed at the low subscriber price of just $2.45 each. That's at least a savings of $3.00 each month below the publishers price. There is never any shipping, handling or other hidden charges. What's more there is no minimum number of books you must buy, you may return any selection for full credit and you can cancel your subscription at any time. A TRUE VALUE!

Mail the coupon below

To start your subscription and receive 2 FREE WESTERNS, fill out the coupon below and mail it today. We'll send you your first shipment which includes 2 FREE BOOKS as soon as we receive it.

J.R. ROBERTS
THE
GUNSMITH